To Maverick –
Merry Christmas 2021!

Listen to the animals!

EIGHT PAWS
TO
GEORGIA

A True
International
Adventure

Warm Wishes,

by Kiska, the Cat

(as told to Pamela Bauer Mueller)

Pamela Bauer Mueller

10/23/2021

PIÑATA PUBLISHING

Piñata Publishing
626 Old Plantation Road
Jekyll Island, GA 31527
912-635-9402

www.pinatapub.com

CANADIAN CATALOGUING IN PUBLICATION
Mueller, Pamela Bauer
    Eight Paws to Georgia

ISBN: 978-09685097-2-2

    1. Cats—Juvenile fiction. Weiler, Naomi. II. Title.
PZ7.B324Ei 2001   J813'.54   C2001-911304-8

Library of Congress Card Number: 2001129249

Typeset by Vancouver Desktop Publishing Centre
Printed and bound in the USA by Patterson Printing

Acknowledgments

Many thanks are due to the following:

The Belt Family: Phil, Kim, Virginia, John and Coco: our first and dearest friends in St. Simons Island. Your spiritual gifts and friendship have enriched our lives.

Nancy Thomason and Daisy, for the enjoyment of your company and the knowledge you provided on the Georgian way of life.

Dr. Lisa Ryan, whose kindness and compassion ministered courage and comfort to Kiska and to me.

Frankie Cox and Roberta Morgan, for compiling your insightful list of "Southern speak" which made possible the writing of the chapter "Georgia Nice."

Brother Don and his wife Wendy, for listening to my heart and soul and holding my hand during Kiska's last days. Thank you for sharing with us your tender tribute to your beloved Oscar during our mourning.

Eleanor and Gary Livingstone, who taught us about donkeys. Thank you for opening your hearts and your home and imparting your love for your animals.

Wynne Toba, for offering us "The Rainbow Bridge Story," and for your quiet wisdom.

Joana Phillips, whose incredible cats, Pansey and Speedy, proved worthy storytellers themselves.

Ellspette Dyer-Green, for appreciating Yoda's astuteness to heal his body, and then presenting it to us.

My daughters, Cassandra Coveney and Ticiana Gordillo, who with their awesome spouses, continue to bring us pride, joy and blessings.

Marlena Grace, our grandbaby, who encourages in us the thrill of regressing to childhood and delighting in its wonders.

Naomi Weiler, my multi-talented friend and illustrator. You bring vibrant life to our imagination! Cheers!

Patty Osborne, our book guru, thank you for your good nature, clever wit, and consistent outstanding work.

Ray Hignell, your cleverness and vast knowledge of book printing has glided us through this trilogy. Kudos to you!

Michael, my beloved husband. Thank you for being my partner. And for loving Kiska in word and deed!

Foreword

Friendship is precious, not only in the shade, but also in the sunshine of life. And thanks to a benevolent arrangement of things, the greater part of life is sunshine.

—Thomas Jefferson

This book is all about belonging. Kiska's final story invites the reader to travel on our journey from western Canada to southeastern United States. With her words, she paints clear pictures and applies her singular insight to everything that she touches. Kiska sets the rules with a domestic policy all her own. She understands that life is a daring adventure, a constant sea of change. She lives hers with a positive attitude and a sparkle of humor.

Kiska's fragments of wisdom will appeal to the aspiration and longing that slumber in our hearts. We were blessed with her sweet friendship for over nineteen years. In this book I have once again climbed inside her skin and listened to her heart.

Thank you, Kiska, for exemplifying that love is the most powerful of all of life's forces.

—Pamela Bauer Mueller

Contents

On the Road Again?

Jasper and I knew that big changes were in the air. Our house was a hub of activity: people coming in and out, cartons packed and stored, furniture wrapped for moving. What we didn't know was "when" it would take place. I had moved several times before and did not like the process. Jasper had never moved, so he was frightened and confused by the strangers, the noise and commotion. He spent a lot of time hiding under the masters' bed.

Then the movers arrived and all of our belongings were carried out of the house and into a very big truck. Three large men hauled out sofas and beds and cartons of dishes. I sat on the edge of the hot tub and watched from a safe distance. Jasper stayed under the bed. When they left the house was empty. The Mistress and Mr. Mike told us they would be staying in a hotel for the night, and we should take care of the house. The next day they would come for us.

While we roamed the big empty house, memories flooded my mind. Cats relive their moments periodically, because we are reflective creatures and enjoy meditating on our good times. My memories drifted all the way back to our days in Mexico.

How far I had come from my early life with this family. It was eighteen years ago that the Mistress, Miss Cassandra and Miss Ticiana selected my brother, Canica, and me from a litter of kittens in Mexico City! We grew up among the sounds and smells of the Mexican culture, enjoying our idyllic lives to the fullest. Then we suddenly moved to San Diego! We were bewildered and caught unaware but we quickly adjusted to a new home and made new friends. One day Canica left us all to live on his own, becoming an animal actor in Los Angeles. I stayed behind with the girls and helped them grow into beautiful ladies.

During those years in San Diego, we experienced two more moves, Miss Cassandra's wedding, and Mr. Mike's entrance into our lives. After eight wonderful years being a California cat, the Mistress told me we would be moving to another country, Canada. At that point, I understood that moving was part of the plan. As long as I stayed with my loved ones, all was well.

Jasper joined our family in Canada. Once again I had an animal partner as well as my human family. We have been living here for six enjoyable years and have shared many adventures. Now I sense that we are about to embark on another journey. Cats have an uncanny knowledge of events to come. Despite my discomfort in leaving behind friends and all things familiar, this time I feel ready to go.

A Slimy Green Coat

The following afternoon we were taken into our first temporary house in White Rock. This living arrangement was called Pier View Bed and Breakfast. A bed and breakfast is where the humans sleep in a rented room and the owners fix them food in the morning. In our case, since the Mistress and Mr. Mike went to work early, the food was left in our refrigerator and they ate it whenever they wanted. We had a wonderful living arrangement there. The large lawn in front had a view of the ocean and the White Rock Pier. The weather was very warm because it was summer time. Jasper and I quickly became comfortable and even shared our area with the dog and cat that lived upstairs.

Kelly the Dog was a friendly yellow lab that studied us from her upstairs terrace. She would stick her neck through the iron fence and watch us sunbathing on our patio. Her master often took her for long walks on the beach. We watched them winding their way down the steep streets as they headed toward the town and the water below. Kelly never pestered us in any way. She actually made us feel welcome as she observed us and shared her beautiful home. Mandy the Cat visited us at times, but preferred to govern her domain from above. She knew we were temporary and chose not to get too attached to us.

One day Jasper and I ventured across the street to explore. We discovered that we could see the ocean even better over there. By now we recognized the smell of our new home, so we could wander a few yards away and still find our way back. We also had to cross a street, which can be very dangerous for a cat, but we were on our guard for cars and enjoyed our outing. When we returned to our new home we stretched out in the patio and slept in the afternoon sun.

Jasper was more impatient to investigate other areas than I was. He was already meeting new cats that lived in the area.

One afternoon he disappeared for quite a while. Finally he came racing across the front yard, crouched low, head bowed and sopping wet! Mr. Mike was in the yard and saw Jasper run under the staircase to hide. He was shivering, looking very humiliated and not wanting to be found. Mr. Mike pulled him out from behind the staircase and realized that Jasper was covered from head to toe with green slime. Finally Mr. Mike realized it was algae, but where did he find algae? Jasper looked at me with such confusion and concern. I just wanted to wash this green stuff off his wet body to help him out. Mr. Mike ran water in the bathtub and gave Jasper a good bath.

Later Jasper told me that he was running across a yard and fell headfirst into a pond, which was covered with green algae so that he could not see the water below! After that adventure, I believe Jasper slowed down and watched where he was running. I know that he never wanted to wear a slimy green coat again!

3

The Donkey House

We stayed at Pier View Bed and Breakfast for about six weeks and then moved on to the "Donkey House." The Donkey House was the home of eleven donkeys, two very large dogs, and two wonderful friends of Mr. Mike and the Mistress, Eleanor and Gary. They lived in a spacious and beautiful home. The property also had a barn for the donkeys, a greenhouse for the plants, and a cottage for their guests. We lived in the cottage, and we loved to sit on the window ledges and watch the birds eat from the outside feeders. The Mistress told me that the windows had special glass;

we could see out but the birds could not see in. The cottage had winding stairs leading up to the bedroom and the office area. The kitchen, dining room and living room were downstairs. This cottage reminded me of the dollhouse that Miss Cassandra and Miss Ticiana had as children.

Miss Cassandra was twelve years old and Miss Ticiana was nine. Their parents bought them a dollhouse for Christmas, big and colorful with four or five rooms. Canica and I played and sometimes slept in the dollhouse. One day we hid our catnip mouse behind the tiny sofa and then knocked the front door over trying to pull it out. As the plastic door fell off, Canica tried to leap over the top to get away. Instead, he skidded into the side door. He braced himself from falling by placing his front paws on top of the roof. The next thing we knew, the plastic house collapsed and we ran away in fright!

As I mentioned earlier, cats thrive on memories. Being students of behavior, we observe, note and absorb the experiences by remembering them again and again. Often our memories turn into catnaps, which may explain why we sleep so often. During our stay in the Donkey House, I spent a great deal of time reflecting on my past.

My brother Canica and I grew up in Mexico, amid the music and laughter of the Latin people. Our neighborhood was in the mountainside above Mexico City. Our house was one of eight in a beautiful tree lined compound. We had flowers, forts, playground equipment and animals everywhere. There were other cats and dogs living there as well as children who adored us. The owners of the compound raised chickens, and we often amused ourselves by sneaking into the chicken coops after the workers left for the day. We grew up bilingual because the Mistress spoke to us in English and everyone else, including Miss Cassandra and Miss Ticiana, spoke to us in Spanish. Those were wonderful, carefree days.

Then we moved to San Diego and left the Master in Mexico. A divorce is a difficult time for everyone involved, including the cats. Canica suffered more than I did because he left a sweetheart in Mexico and never really forgot her. He ran away as soon as we arrived in California, but fortunately I found him that same night. Almost a year later he set out on his own, leaving us for his new life in Los Angeles to become an animal actor. One day the Mistress and I saw him on a television cat food commercial, so we knew he had found his niche. I am happy for him, but I miss him even today.

The girls had grown up and moved away by the time we once again relocated. The Mistress, Mr. Mike, and I drove up in her small convertible to White Rock, a small seaside village in British Columbia, Canada. That is where we settled for the next six years. Miss Ticiana was attending the University of Oregon and she came home often. How we looked forward to her visits! Miss Cassandra was married and eventually had a little baby girl, Marlena Grace. They visited us in White Rock, so again our home was filled with laughter, the Spanish language and happy moments.

Now we're in the process of another move; this one is to Georgia. The Mistress tells me that Georgia is in the South and the weather is usually warm. That sounds good to me, because I'm becoming an old lady, at least in years. I will be nineteen on October 10, which is around the time we will move. I do hope this is the last move for a while. This time, instead of moving with Canica I'm moving with Jasper. Jasper adopted us during our stay in White Rock, and has become my best buddy. He's so much like Canica, yet very much his own cat. Life has been so much better for all of us since he came to live with us.

Now we're exploring new territories in this cottage, watching the birds and avoiding the big dogs. I go outside with the Mistress or Mr. Mike, but Jasper is very frightened of the dogs. Soon you will understand why!

Down the Ladder

The dogs, Leah and Sheba, are of the large Bouvier des Flandres breed. Eleanor explained their origin to my Mistress, but all I remember is their unusual name. To me they appeared huge and black. They have a loud and menacing bark, probably meant for herding and protection. The day that we arrived at the cottage the Mistress took us outdoors to become acquainted with the area. Instantly we heard tremendous growls coming from inside the big house, followed by thundering barks. Both of us shot back through the cottage door and darted under the bed. We would have loved to explore the pond and expansive yard and flowers, but we so feared the noise of the dogs that we never ventured out again unless the masters were right there to protect us.

I was somewhat less terrified than Jasper. I knew that if the Mistress or Mr. Mike were with me I would be safe. Jasper doubted their powers. Every afternoon one of them would return from work and take us out for sun and fresh air. Jasper usually waited about thirty seconds and then raced up the side wood panel of the cottage to the roof, from where he could launch himself through the upstairs window into the safety of the bedroom. I walked among the flowers

31

and sat by the pond watching the ducks, making sure from the corner of my eye that one of the masters was within sight.

Late one afternoon Mr. Mike was able to convince Jasper to stay outdoors for several minutes. As the dogs were off on a walk with their owners, we heard no threatening howls from the house. I sensed that Jasper was relaxing and beginning to enjoy himself, sniffing out the new odors and observing the ducks at a closer distance. I wandered over to the greenhouse and was about to enter when I heard such a commotion! The dogs had returned and en route to their house realized that we were outside. With a loud bark of excitement, they bounded to the yard where Jasper had been exploring. Jasper, quick as a flash, tore up the closest tree. His hair was standing on end and he had wild fear in his eyes. Up he scrambled, higher and higher, until he felt safe. I scurried back to the cottage, out of harm's way.

The dogs stood guard at the tree until Gary pulled them away. Jasper stayed in the tree for quite some time. Mr. Mike told the Mistress he wanted to give him time to calm down. He then got an enormous ladder from Gary, climbed up to pry Jasper's claws from the bark, and carried him down. Mr. Mike had to descend backwards, with his buttocks bumping the rails of the ladder so he could keep a two handed grip on Jasper. Jasper placed his front paws around Mr. Mike's neck and buried his head under Mr. Mike's chin during the trip down the ladder. He later told me that his heart was pumping so loudly that he thought it might pop out. I watched this with alarm from my spot on the windowsill.

Both Eleanor and Gary explained to us that the dogs simply wanted to play. We couldn't consider that as an option and never gave them another opportunity. We discussed this and mutually decided to become "indoor cats" the duration of our stay in that cottage.

Visits and Surprises

The Mistress was retiring from her job with U.S. Customs at the same time that Mr. Mike received a promotion to teach at the Federal Law Enforcement Training Center in Georgia. I know all of this because I eavesdrop. "Eavesdrop" means to listen to other people's conversations when you are not invited to do so. Cats are very good at this custom. We just pretend to be asleep and gather all sorts of information. Because the Mistress was retiring, a large party was being planned. Mr. Mike shared with us a forthcoming surprise that would make her very happy!

The Mistress knew that Miss Ticiana would be coming in from Oregon for the party, but Miss Cassandra had told her that she could not make it from far away Minnesota because of work. The Mistress understood and knew she would see them for Thanksgiving. Mr. Mike had secretly arranged (in the same bed and breakfast where we had lived) to lodge both girls, Dan and baby Marlena. The afternoon they arrived, Mr. Mike went to the airport to pick them up. Jasper and I perched on the windowsill with a good view of the car as it drove up. The Mistress rushed outside to meet Miss Ticiana. To her shock and delight, the other three climbed out of the back seat. The Mistress burst into tears of happiness, causing the others to weep as well. Jasper and I felt very proud to have been privy to this delightful surprise!

That weekend we sat outside on the rooftop, doing surveillance on the whole lot. We enjoyed watching Eleanor, Gary, the Mistress, Mr. Mike and all the visitors play with the donkeys. These donkeys love human contact. They brayed happily as little Marlena, standing high on her tiptoes rubbed their necks, kissing and hugging them where she could reach. All animals feel a strong bond towards people

who love them. Little children without fear touch a tender spot in all of us.

The donkeys pranced about as they were allowed to leave their corral area and graze in the immense yard. As they drew nearer to us, we retreated inside and continued to watch them from the windowsill. Jasper and I made it a game to see who could memorize their names first. I won. I'll share their names with you: Bonnie, Buttons, Cinders, Jasmine, Jessie, Jill, Moondust, Sabrina, Symba, Taffy, and Wee Willy. I think I won because I alphabetized them in my brain, so it was easier to pull them up on demand. After we became accustomed to hearing their braying morning, noon, night and sometimes at dawn, we felt a certain kinship with them. As far as "other than cat" favorite animal species goes, donkeys are high on my list!

The girls left after the party weekend and the Mistress's mother, Phyllis, arrived for a short holiday. We cats had a nice visit with her while the masters worked. She is a very sweet lady and allowed us to sleep with her, so she earned a special place in our hearts. During this time I noticed that we began to pack up everything again. Some items were going directly into the car. The Mistress and Mr. Mike playfully argued about how many plants could ride with us, so I knew that we were finally ready to depart for this new place: the state of Georgia. As much as I dislike car trips, I was ready to leave this "Dog and Donkey Show" and find a place of our own.

Like a Tourist

Early one October morning we drove away from Canada. I could tell by the silence in the car that each of us was privately saying a sad "good-bye" to a wonderful country. Our experiences and our friends there would be valued forever in our hearts. We crossed the border into Blaine, Washington where Mr. Mike had worked for five years. Then we drove eastward through the state of Washington and into Idaho. I have all this knowledge because I pay close attention to details and I wanted you to know the specifics of our move to the south.

Naturally I protested the car trip, as I always do. But this time it was better because both Jasper and I were in the soft-sided cat carrier. I could snuggle up to him to sleep and he could comfort me with his purring and bathing. The car was again packed to the brim, reminding me of the move from San Diego to Vancouver. But now I had a companion cat and that seemed to help my motion sickness. We quietly conversed in the back seat and Jasper soothed my nerves. Each time the Mistress turned around to inquire about our state of being I felt obligated to meow in disapproval to let her know that this was not fun!

After a few hours the masters found a motel and unpacked for the night. Now the fun began! Jasper and I were eager to explore our new quarters and quickly surveyed the room. Jasper loved to look at himself in the mirror. He would stand up, stretch to his full height with his paws on the glass, and admire himself. This he did in every motel room between Vancouver and Georgia. The masters even took photos of him doing this because they found it so endearing. I hurried to discover all the nooks and crannies where we could hide out when they wanted to put us back into the cat carrier. These activities added a touch of entertainment to our daily travels.

After several days of traveling we arrived at Yellowstone National Park. They carried us into a homey log cabin and told us that we would be staying there for three days. The next day it began to snow, and we enjoyed sitting at the windowsill and observing the falling snowflakes. We were comfortably warm inside and wondered why the Mistress and Mr. Mike were walking and playing outside in the cold. They told us that Yellowstone National Park was famous for its geysers, mud pots, thermal hot springs, mineral deposits and wildlife. Since they had such a short time to explore all of this, they were gone most of the day and sometimes into the night.

On a night that we were alone, we watched with amazement as three deer ventured up our steps looking for food. Their dark eyes glowed and their hooves clicked as they stepped on the landing. Jasper told me that he also saw a skunk and a small bear, but I must have been sleeping.

When the three days were over we piled back into the car. I still protested now and again, but I was actually comfortable and almost enjoyed the ride. When I felt stiff and needed a change, I climbed up on Jasper's back and rode there for a time. Then I might roll down on my back, with my feet extended straight up, touching the ceiling of the carrier. Jasper accepted whatever I wanted to do. He is so easy going that it is hard to annoy him. I don't think he complained once the whole trip across the country.

"M" is For Mary

I noticed that I was feeling more tired than usual. I was also urinating more often. Before we left Canada the Mistress had my blood tested. The vet found that my kidneys were functioning at a less than normal rate. The vet put a blood pressure cuff on my front leg and discovered that my blood pressure was also low. The Mistress began to give me daily medication and changed my food to a lower protein version so it would be easier to digest. At that time I was feeling just fine, but now I realized that I felt tired, even from sleeping in the car. Maybe it was just the traveling?

Perhaps you don't know this but I am the runt of my litter. That means that I was the smallest at birth and probably remained smaller than my siblings throughout life. According to the Mistress, being the runt accounts for my elevated intelligence. Some people believe that smaller dogs and cats outlive larger ones. I do know that I just had my nineteenth birthday, and according to the people who discuss my age in front of me, nineteen seems to be a very long time for a cat to live. Since I am planning on living a while longer, I guess people don't always know as much as they think about cats.

I am a tabby cat. We tabby cats wear many colors in our fur coats, but usually we have some grey, brown, black and white mixed in there. We often have broad black stripes on our backs. Some of us have long hair; others, like me, have short hair. I have heard us referred to as "alley cats" or "European domestic" cats. All of us have a dark "m" mark on our foreheads, situated between our eyes and above our nose. Even cats with tabby coloring only on the face may carry the "m." One day the Mistress heard a very compassionate story about how we received that special marking.

Many years ago, when baby Jesus was born, his

mother Mary called the barnyard animals to her. She asked them to gather close to help keep Jesus warm. The larger cattle and sheep obediently lay down by the manger while the camels huddled nearby. The small tabby cat jumped into the manger and curled up next to the baby. Soon Mary noticed that baby Jesus began to glow with the cat's warmth. A grateful Mary leaned over the cat and blessed him with the sign of the cross on his forehead. Joseph later exclaimed with surprise that the letter "m" was imprinted on the fur of the cat's forehead. The "M" for Mary has remained as a mark on our foreheads from that day on.

I like to believe that the Virgin Mary blessed all tabby cats with that loving gesture.

Eight Paws to Georgia

We were driving across the country and reached North Dakota. Jasper and I were taken out of the car for a break in Theodore Roosevelt National Park. It was a land of vast silent spaces, with plains and colorful canyons everywhere. Mr. Mike told us that water and wind have sculpted the canyons, which are called the Badlands. I was very impressed with the desert beauty!

The next night we arrived in Minneapolis, Minnesota, where Miss Cassandra, Dan and baby Marlena live. We stayed in a motel, but they came by immediately to visit us. It was so wonderful seeing Miss

Cassandra again. She tucked me into her arms as she always did and cooed lovingly to me. She also gave Jasper a hug and a quick pet, before he dove under the bed. Small children and strangers still frighten him, and he finds refuge under furniture. After a while the masters left with them, giving Jasper and me another motel room to explore. We stayed in this area for several days, so they could spend time with the family. Jasper and I were very content to stay in one place!

I felt my energy return each time I stayed somewhere more than one night. Every morning either the Mistress or Mr. Mike had to stick a big pill on the back of my tongue and rub my throat so I would swallow it. This was my medication, and we all disliked the procedure. I knew they were doing what was best for me, so I allowed it to happen. But once in a while I would only pretend to swallow it, and then moments later they would discover that pill on the bed cover or the floor.

From Minnesota we traveled on to Wisconsin, where we briefly visited Mr. Mike's mother, Jeane. Then we headed for Dixon, Illinois. The Mistress and Mr. Mike met up with more relatives there: Aunt Betty, Uncle Ray, Cousin Jon and his wife, Joy. We also spent a night in Carbondale, Illinois and met the Mistress's niece, Miss Jill. She was very affectionate to both Jasper and me.

You may wonder how I know all these names and places. To get the facts, I simply need to employ my four avenues of investigation: eyes, ears, nose and whiskers. You will see just how much we cats pick up when we pay attention. I'm getting very good with names now, even if I only meet people briefly. Maybe I like to challenge myself with this skill. Jasper seems to have no interest, but he is not writing a book either. I also learned to appreciate these stops that we made. I discovered that when the masters spend time with their friends and family, Jasper and I are allowed a great deal of unsupervised time. This turned out to be a very good thing. It also meant less time in the car and more time resting in a hotel, which we definitely prefer.

As we left Illinois, I began to hear the Mistress speak excitedly about a place called Graceland. This is the home of a very famous singer, Elvis Presley, located in Memphis, Tennessee. The Mistress had been looking forward to visiting this place for a long time. She convinced Mr. Mike that he would love it as well. It was a bit out of the way from our travel plans, but they decided to go there anyway. We arrived on a warm, humid afternoon. They parked in the shade and left the windows partially down for Jasper and me. They spent the afternoon exploring this famous home, but the Mistress returned to the car several times to check on us. When we left Graceland they were both chatting with pleasure,

so we realized that Mr. Mike liked it very much indeed.

Late the next afternoon we arrived in St. Simons Island, Georgia, which would be our new home. Our traveling days were over! We were so happy to be able to walk into our rented cottage and know that we would be staying there until we found a house to buy. It was a wonderful feeling to realize that we were here! Georgia would be our new place to live and it looked very welcoming. The day was warm, the ocean was nearby, and the smells were marvelous. I closed my eyes and said a little prayer of thanks.

"Georgia Nice"

It didn't take Jasper and me more than two days to realize that things were very different in Georgia. First of all, it was warm! This was the end of October, and we could be outside all day and be warmed by the sun. Our little rental home was close enough to the ocean for us to hear and smell the salty waves, which was a real treat. Talk about relaxation! Once again we set out to familiarize ourselves with the new neighborhood, the animals, and the people.

The first cat we met in Georgia was Daisy. The Mistress had been to a bookstore in the village and

met the cat who lived there. Then she took us to meet her. Daisy looked very much like Jasper, but she had most unusual paw pads. Most cats with a large amount of white fur have pink paw pads; darker cats have black pads. Jasper is white with black patches so he has pink paw pads. Daisy is also white with black patches, but she has some pink pads, some black pads, and some mixed pink and black paw pads! Her Mistress, a very pleasant cat person named Nancy, introduced us and soon we were following Daisy around her store. We had made our first new feline friend!

The people were very sociable and kind to us. As always, we encouraged them to pamper us. I noticed that they were harder to understand than our friends on the West Coast. They spoke in a soft soothing coastal way, and they pronounced their words differently. Sometimes Jasper and I didn't know what they had just said to us, but we smiled with our "moon eyes" (slits of catly ecstasy), lowered our heads for rubbing and urged them to scratch our tummies anyway.

One day I heard the Mistress and Mr. Mike talking about the new Georgian words they were learning. They were impressed and charmed with the delightful phrases they heard, so I took it upon myself to memorize some of them to share with y'all (you). That's the very first expression I heard the first time I ventured out. Since then, here is a sampling of other Georgian talk, which is a main ingredient of the "Georgia nice" attitude here.

"Fixin' to" means you are going to do something.
"Youngens" are children.
"Dawg" is dog.
"Bay ah" is the two syllable word for bear (which I thought was a one syllable word).
"Pee cans" is pecans, which make up my Mistress's favorite pie!
"Hush up" means to be quiet.
"Yawn to" means do you want to?
"Poe leese" is police.
"Cut your eye at" means to look at.
"Jeet yet?" means "Did you eat yet?"
"Far" means fire.
"Ah" is I.
"Fussin at" is scolding someone.
"Rastlin" means wrestling.

And my personal favorite is "Joe Jah" which, naturally, is the correct pronunciation of Georgia! There are many more, but I have shared my favorites with you.

We quickly learned that the Georgian people are very cordial. They do everything with a smile and always call out a greeting to you, whether they know you or not. They are also very polite, and the children are taught to say "Yes Ma'am" and "Yes Sir" to the adults. Each evening the Mistress and Mr. Mike would share their day's experiences, while Jasper and I would lay at their feet and absorb this new culture. It was great fun to learn as they educated themselves, and we practiced the pronunciation when they were out of hearing range.

Some of the food they eat here is different and truly delicious, even to a cat. On occasions we were able to sample some new food items. The local people love grits, greens (collard, spinach, and mustard), pig tails and hog jowls, chitterlings, yellow or red rice, hush puppies, cathead biscuits (so big they can choke a cat), sweet iced tea, slaw dogs (cole slaw on hot dogs), boiled peanuts, okra, fried catfish and black-eyed peas. Please don't ask me to describe each of these. I only just learned the names from overhearing my masters' conversations.

The trees and sea animals of St. Simons Island are

also totally new to us. Here we found lovely twisted live oak trees hundreds of years old, with bluish green moss dangling off the branches. We discovered cypress and dogwood trees, as well as gum trees and hickories. We recognized many types of pine trees, and palm tree varieties that we knew from San Diego living. When Jasper and I ventured out to the beach, we saw the most magnificent seashells. Sometimes they still had living creatures inside! During our first two weeks here, the Mistress brought home and pointed out to us angel wings, jingles, whelks, moon shells, cockles, slipper shells and sand dollars.

So it was with great excitement that Jasper and I studied the new area. Different words, new landscaping and totally fresh smells for us to absorb gave us immense pleasure. We were like young children at Christmas time, awakening every day in anticipation of another new surprise! Our first two weeks were a constant thrill as we discovered the treasures of Georgia.

Companionship

"Finally, all of you, live in harmony with one another; be sympathetic, love as brothers, be compassionate and humble.

—1 Peter 3:8

Sometimes I spend time reflecting on my relationship with my family. I wonder if all cats are as fortunate as I am. Most of the cats I've questioned tell me that they communicate with their humans, but not to the extent that I do with the Mistress. My two new cat neighbors, Abbey and Nip, use verbal commands with their masters. They voice a "mow" to suggest snuggling in their beds, and a "miaw-rrow" when they want the litter box changed. Jasper and I have our catly phrases as well, but our true communication runs much deeper.

I think our ability to "converse" beyond the norm is based on mutual respect. The Mistress has always been owned by cats and has taught everyone around her to respect our dignity. She never speaks down to a cat. She explains everything and allows us to use our intelligence to understand as a human would. Because she can imagine a part of herself into a cat, we cats quickly realize what she wishes through observation. I also make my needs clear to her through her powers of perception. When I make a sound, it is usually to reinforce her actions, and to praise her.

A companion is a comrade and a partner in a long-term relationship. I have enjoyed companionship with two cats, Canica and Jasper, and a few humans. Miss Cassandra selected me from a litter of kittens, and she was my first beloved companion. She loved me and showed me what love means. We shared adventures and sorrows, and helped each other through the difficult transitions that life assigned to us. Miss Ticiana cared for both Canica and me throughout her growing up years. When Miss

Cassandra left for college, I comforted Miss Ticiana and kept her feet warm under the covers. She also holds a very special place in my heart.

My dear brother, Canica, was by my side for almost four years. We shared such exciting adventures, both in Mexico and in San Diego! But Canica needed to live an extraordinary life, and his restlessness took him to Los Angeles, California, where he became an animal actor. We proudly watch his commercials and realize that he's found his niche.

Mr. Mike entered my world when I was a "mature lady," and has offered me his affection and esteem ever since. He makes sure that our claws are trimmed and our coats are brushed. Mr. Mike likes to include us in the family outings, and will often take us for rides about town. Above all, I will forever be grateful to him for giving the Mistress his love and support.

Just four years ago, Jasper landed in our home with a bang and captivated all of us with his charm. Although I taught him ordinary procedures and how to appreciate our masters, he soon became the leader in our adventures. He values my seniority and honors my status as "matriarch." Jasper is noble and generous and loves us unconditionally.

However, my companion throughout the ages has

been the Mistress. She has seen me through all the changes, the good times and bad times. It is to her that I turn when my energy fails and my body tires. She knows when I need to be held and kissed, just as I understand and comfort her during her sad and discouraging moments. The Mistress recognizes the cat's grace and intelligence, she encourages its independence, she adores its dignity. Companionship is a special commendation awarded to those who trust one another.

Glows in the Dark

By early November we had settled nicely in our cottage by the sea. Mr. Mike enjoyed teaching physical technique classes at the Federal Law Enforcement Training Center (FLETC) and the Mistress was learning all she could about the area. One evening she announced with great enthusiasm that she had arranged for all of us to go on a shrimp boat. Our ears perked up when we realized that we were included in this expedition on water. Several years ago they had taken us on a two hour ferry boat trip to visit Vancouver Island, but this sounded like something entirely different.

That Saturday we were awakened very early and carried into the car in our cat carrier. After a short drive across the causeway, we reached the Brunswick waterfront marina. Stretching our necks from inside our carrier we could see several large boats side by side. They looked about sixty feet long and had rounded bottoms, flared fronts and square tails. The masters left us in the car while they spoke to two men, who turned out to be the crew of our shrimp boat. Jasper and I were nervously watching the choppy seawaters, wishing we were asleep back at the cottage. As Mr. Mike carried us onboard, The Mistress whispered to us that this would be an exciting adventure.

Once onboard, we pulled away from the dock and moved along the Turtle River. The Captain explained to the masters the history of the shrimp and how they catch them. He probably didn't realize that Jasper and I were listening and learning as well. I'll bet he was wondering just why we were there on his boat, but he was too polite to ask.

We learned that the shrimp has twenty legs, swims backwards and forwards, and glows in the dark! The Captain explained that adult shrimp spawn close to the beaches in May. The babies are then swept

inshore to spend the summer in the beautiful nutrient-rich salt marshes. This area of Georgia is filled with marshlands, which I will describe to you at a later time. By early fall, the fully-grown shrimp begin their departure to the open sea. We were headed out to find them.

As we traveled out to open sea, we passed the village of St. Simons and Jasper and I saw the gleaming white lighthouse. As we sailed past, the Captain gave us a brief history class on the area. This lighthouse is St. Simon's second one, because the first (built in 1810) was destroyed during the Civil War. This one is 106 feet tall, with 129 steps to the top. He told us that it is a working lighthouse and its light is visible 23 miles out to sea. The Mistress had described it to us but it was truly magnificent from the water!

We rode past the pier and could see people with their lines and shrimp traps, fishing from the sides. Directly opposite we saw the pristine white beaches of Jekyll Island stretching on for miles. Mr. Mike told us that Jekyll Island has an interesting history involving the rich and famous.

Now we were entering the rougher waters off the coast, headed to our destination of about five miles offshore. As we sailed along these waters, Jasper nudged me to look back. Two large dolphins burst out of the water right behind our boat! The Mistress had also spotted them and shared this news with the others. They followed us for a few moments, teasing us with their nearness and graceful leaps. We had never seen dolphins before, so this was an added pleasure for Jasper and me.

The shrimp boat came to a slow stop, and the crew told us that this was the area where they would throw the two large nets. They also would drop a noisy tickler chain to frighten the shrimp into the nets. Although there are three major species of shrimp fished commercially in these waters, we would be catching mostly white shrimp on this trip. Brown shrimp are also found around here, and pink shrimp live in areas with rocky bottoms.

The masters found this all very fascinating, but Jasper and I soon lost interest and began to doze off, lulled by the movement of the boat. At one point I heard Mr. Mike asking about baiting, which involves mixing mud and bait into a ball and throwing it into the water. As the shrimp feed on the fishmeal, the cast net is thrown over the area where the bait is. It seemed that this crew used several methods to locate and catch the shrimp.

Some time later a wide-eyed Jasper was nudging my face to wake me up. Surrounded by happy shouts and the slapping sounds of nets being emptied on the back deck, we watched as hundreds of shrimp and other small creatures were released into the contained area. The shrimp were separated and the rest of the catch was returned to the sea. At one point, Jasper pushed his paw on the mesh siding of the carrier so he could touch the shrimp. As they recoiled and faced him, he quickly withdrew it!

We watched with total interest as the shrimp were quickly de-headed by pinching the head where it joins the body. Then they were placed on ice. You can imagine the wonderful aroma of fresh seafood that permeated the air! But alas, we were not fed any of it. Much later, back at the cottage, the Mistress presented us with a small portion of the six hundred-pound catch of the day!

After what seemed like many hours of consistent boat noises, we sailed back to the dock. The masters took us to the car and returned to watch the shrimp cleaning process. Jasper and I were happy to be back on land, and promptly fell asleep. We later agreed that our first shrimping trip definitely met our expectations.

Cat Yarns

One of the perks of being a writer is that everyone tells you his/her story. In my case, the cat friends I've made share their tales with me. I think that you might like to hear some of my favorite ones, so I've dedicated this chapter to cat tales. These three stories were told at Cat Council, which is a meeting of the cats' minds that Jasper and I attended in White Rock, British Columbia. We are hoping to start one here in Georgia, but first we must get settled into our new neighborhood.

While living in British Columbia, we made friends with a cat named Pansey. He told us that he liked to hide in the mornings so he wouldn't be put outside while his family was away for the day. After they left he jumped to the windowsill and waited for them to return, watching the world go by. One morning he badly misjudged his choice of a hiding place and ended up in the refrigerator! Knowing it would be a long wait, and being rather lazy by nature, Pansey decided to curl up and sleep until they came home.

Upon returning that afternoon, his family called him and searched everywhere but could not find him. Rushing around frantically, they began to look in strange places, finally opening the refrigerator door. To their surprise and horror, Pansey was lying on the bottom shelf! He was in a deep sleep, perhaps a coma, and could not be awakened. The family wrapped him in warm towels, placed him on the car floor next to the heater and rushed to the vet. With the heat blasting on his body, he woke up just as they arrived at the vet's office. According to Pansey, he did not panic or meow and kept himself calm. Only through this relaxation was he able to conserve the oxygen in the refrigerator and not suffocate. That story impressed us all and taught us to conserve energy whenever possible.

I have nothing against the canine species. I simply think that we felines are superior! But I have a story

R ICE

71

that illustrates how we can accommodate them as "staff". Speedy, another friend of ours, related how her housemate, Midas the Dog, assisted her in the birth of her kittens. Speedy gave birth often, and each time she counted on Midas's help to clean and care for her kittens. Midas always obliged, and the kittens grew up thinking he was their Papa. It was he who rescued them when they fell into ditches or tumbled down stairs, because his mouth was so large that he could pick up more than one at a time. Speedy told us that he was her best friend!

My last story involves my friend Yoda, who also joined us in White Rock at our frequent Cat Councils. Yoda adopted a wonderful couple who came looking for a kitten at the local Humane Society in Burnaby, British Columbia. He had the face of a lynx and the body of a raccoon with a glorious bushy ring marked tail. He also had the sniffles. After moving in with his family, it became obvious that Yoda was not well. He sneezed often to try to remove the nasty mucous from his lungs and his eyes wept constantly. He hadn't eaten for days and his owners feared that he would leave them soon.

His Mistress was a healing therapist who worked with humans. She realized that she must focus on healing Yoda, using all the skills that she had been taught over the years. Just as I've told you many times that animals and humans communicate, she connected with him through meditation and telepathy. She told him that they loved him dearly and needed him to be involved in his own healing process. He told us that she used every procedure that she knew: massage, aromatherapy, crystals and healing energy. In order to make the oils absorb into his system quickly, she set up a vaporizer nearby. Then she massaged the oils into the inside of his ears for fast absorption. With her quartz, she relieved him of discomfort and replaced it with positive energy. By massaging his spine and using the Reiki healing method, she was able to sooth him and gave his physical body the opportunity to repair itself.

The next morning Yoda awoke with clear eyes, no sneezes and an intense hunger. He ate and then ate some more. His masters were dumbstruck. Was it spontaneous healing, a coincidence or a miracle? It seems that only Yoda, the "Wise One", knows the answer.

House Hunting

It was November now and the days were still warm. The nights were cooling off, and the neighbors were talking about a cold front moving in. Some days a little rain fell, but after the constant rain we were accustomed to in British Columbia, this was nothing. Jasper and I spent most of our time outdoors, exploring and napping in the warm sunny afternoons.

The Mistress was spending her time finding us a new home. She and her realtor friend Klickie drove all over the island to see various houses on the market. She entertained us with humorous stories of their adventures. Sometimes she got so excited that she insisted that Mr. Mike go see a house that very evening! Jasper and I exchanged non-concerned glances, knowing that when the right house came along, we would approve.

Both the Mistress and Mr. Mike were taking history classes about coastal Georgia, so we were treated with informational tidbits from time to time. We learned that Georgia became the thirteenth colony of the United Sates in 1733. An Englishman named James Oglethorpe, who fought the Spaniards to claim British rights over the land, settled it. The masters told us about the native Americans who had lived here even before that time, and promised to take us on some field trips to see historical monuments.

Toward the end of November the masters left us for four days while they visited Miss Cassandra, Dan and baby Marlena in Minnesota. As usual, they explained where they would be and when they would return, and left us to be on our best behavior. Because we did not know the neighborhood cats well enough to invite them over, we behaved. I was also feeling tired and a bit weak. I'm sure it was because of the so-called "progressive kidney failure" that the vet had diagnosed. Nevertheless, we enjoyed ourselves and even took long walks under the full moon, scattering fiddler crabs as we walked over the packed sand. Regressing to our kitten stage, we tried skipping in tune with the roar of the ocean and dancing to the mournful cries of the seagulls. We agreed that we were very fortunate cats to be living in such a balmy and beautiful place.

In early December, the Mistress took Mr. Mike to one particular house to visit for the second time. They returned in a state of excitement, realizing that this was the house they wanted. They told us it had a very large front and back yard, and that there was a lake behind the house with a dock and a boat. That sounded good to us, because it meant lots of critters and new bird species to discover. They made an offer on the house, and it was accepted. We were now the owners of our first Southern home!

We moved into our new house four days before Christmas. Jasper and I wanted to go outside immediately, but the masters had a different opinion on that matter. Instead, we were forced to hide in closets while the furniture was unloaded and boxes were unpacked. After several days of living in this manner, we were allowed to discover our new territory.

To our delight, we found this place even more beautiful than the last one near the ocean. I stepped outside and walked toward the lake, warmed by winter sunlight under moss tangled oak trees. Squirrels bustled about everywhere, frogs croaked from under the lily pads, snakes slithered through the long grass and Jasper and I realized that we had found Cats' Paradise. Yes, we were quickly enjoying the perks of the Southern cats!

The Marshlands

Christmas Day had come and gone while the masters unpacked and we cats hid. They remembered to get us a Christmas gift however. Late Christmas afternoon the mistress handed us two small wrapped packages with tiny bows. Jasper tried to open his with his mouth and I didn't even try. Finally Mr. Mike opened them and showed us our new silver identification tags, engraved with our names and new telephone number. No catnip, no treats—we were disappointed. This was an unusual and strange Christmas, to be sure.

We were discovering more about our new area: St.

Simons Island. One afternoon the Mistress packed us up in the cat carrier and drove us out to see the marshlands. She told us that we had to know just how important the marshlands are to all who live here. This island is surrounded by marshland, which means that much of our soil is waterlogged and covered with rushes, cattails and other tall grasses. The Mistress told us that Georgia hosts two-thirds of the marshlands in the eastern United States. She is taking classes on the history and ecology of coastal Georgia and she likes to share these interesting tidbits with Jasper and me. So, armed with her new book of bird species, we settled down on the grassy bank to admire our environment.

The tide was coming in as we watched the tops of the grasses sway with the current and listened to the gentle splashing of the tidal flow. Jasper and I could hardly distinguish between the grass and the water, with the green of one intensifying the blue brown of the other. The Mistress explained to us that the tides flush the silt and debris washed into the marsh from the inland rivers out to the sea. Twice daily there is an influx of tidal flow, bringing the microscopic organisms that many creatures need for nourishment and also the water that they need for their oxygen.

Sitting next to the marshlands, I felt their quiet, changeable beauty. From her classes the Mistress shared with us that the marshlands are the most productive land acre per acre on this planet. With their wealth of nutrients, they support large populations of fish, shellfish, plants, and bird life. Here in their grasses and shallow waters many marine species, like shrimp and clams, begin their lives protected from predators. That afternoon we watched as fiddler crabs scurried across the mud flats and ate decaying vegetation. When the tide went out later that evening, the marsh would appear as a land of tall grasses. Raccoons and other animals would then look for crabs and shellfish.

Jasper and I enjoy the marshlands because they give us wonderful critters to chase and provide entertainment. To give you an example, I'll tell you about our experience with the birds. That first afternoon at the marsh we witnessed a sandpiper dance. She seemed to slide over the land as if moved by the pulse of the water stirring through the salt marsh. The Mistress interrupted our quiet contemplation by excitedly pointing out an osprey diving into the golden grasses. Such a magnificent bird! That image will be forever implanted in my memory.

That afternoon we were treated to a variety of sweet sounding birdcalls. Jasper and I can now identify the cackle of the marsh hen as she fusses at our approach. The marshlands also introduced us to the red wing, allowing us to admire her beauty as she flew overhead, the chestnut-red feathers shining under her wings. As we were leaving the marshland the Mistress' voice startled several ricebirds from their hiding places deep in the reeds. We learned the name

of these birds through the pictures in the bird book the Mistress had brought along with us.

We've always known about some bird species, but never have we been able to study a woodpecker up close. In St. Simons we have pileated woodpeckers living in our back yard. With their beautiful red crests and incessant hammering, they provide us with hours of entertainment. We lay under shaded bushes and watch them chipping off whole shingles from the pine trees. Then we stretch, amble lazily to the tree and meow, causing them to swoop away, shrieking in indignation. At night we often hear the lonely call of the chuck-will's-widow, a solitary bird with a haunting cry. On a daily basis we deal with the racket of the blackbirds as they challenge us to a duel.

15

Frogs, Squirrels, Turtles 'n Gators

One of my favorite sounds is the early evening croaking and whistling of the marsh frogs. These critters come right up into our backyard, where the chase begins and we always lose. Would that be because of the little bells that the masters have secured to our collars? Long ago we realized that the chase is more fun than the catch!

Speaking of the chase, our yard is home to many annoying squirrels. They tease us unmercifully, so we have to respond. First we do the crouch, where not a muscle moves, whiskers bristle and the nose slightly trembles. Then the hindquarters begin to shake and shiver, our tails arch back and forth, and we spring! Jasper and I have never yet caught a squirrel, but we certainly give them a run for their money!

Our second afternoon in the new house, Jasper hurried to my side to tell me about the turtle in the back yard. These turtles live in the lake and often venture up the banks into our yards. This particular turtle was large, but we've seen all sizes. They are friendly enough, but draw their heads into their shells when we get close enough to smell them. So far we've not been able to teach them to play with us.

The Mistress sits on the dock in the late afternoon with dog food. She bangs on the side of the boat with her heels, throws small bits of dog food into the lake, and waits for them to surface and eat. The past owner of the house taught her this ritual, which works very well. I've counted eight to ten turtles of all sizes at one time, eagerly awaiting an opportunity to gobble the food.

One creature we never expected to see up close is the alligator! Nobody told us that from time to time alligators have been spotted in these neighborhoods, so last week Jasper and I had the fright of our lives! Because we overheard conversations about Okefenokee Swamp, we knew that Georgian alligators live in

swampy areas, rivers, streams and ponds. We live next to a lake and never expected to see an alligator here.

One evening we were amusing ourselves next door in Rob and Susie's back yard. We sat at the edge of the lake, balancing on small tree branches and batting at tiny fish with our paws. Without any warning I heard a rustle nearby, like a large animal moving slowly through the leaves. We quickly backed off the branches and scrambled up a small gum tree. It was dark, but we could see two large yellow almond-shaped eyes glaring up at us. Judging from its size, this was not a raccoon or an armadillo. It was a very long dark reptile, moving with a swagger and very slowly shifting its heavy tail from side to side in an intimidating gesture. We raced further up the tree, and there we stayed until we watched it amble slowly back into the lake.

We don't know if cats are "alligator bait," but we have a dreadful suspicion that we are!

At Home at Last

I was losing my appetite and that disturbed me. Jasper actually left me the best of the food selections and I had to force myself to nibble at them. The masters commented on my weight loss and I could see it worried them. So I snuggled in their laps or lay next to their faces and purred loudly. And I slept a lot. I began to dream a great deal during those catnaps. Dreams are why cats sleep so much. We cats can travel back in time and visit our loved ones by directing our thoughts a few seconds before we sleep.

Many of the dreams took place in Mexico. I was

chasing my brother Canica and playing with the girls when they were young. In these dreams Miss Ticiana appeared to be about eight and Miss Cassandra eleven, which is interesting because those were their ages when we adopted them. Canica and I frolicked through the fields and played hide and seek with the young girls. We invaded the chicken coops and darted away from the grasp of those trying to stop us. Sometimes we were running over the rocks beside the streams in beautiful Valle de Bravo, where we had our weekend home. These were dreams of serenity and peace and happiness. I always awoke feeling refreshed.

Jasper knew that I was not feeling well, so he looked after me as never before. He bathed me several times a day, he coaxed me outside when I would rather sleep, and he accompanied me everywhere I went. If I needed water and couldn't find it, he led me to the lake or the fountain on the dock. I seemed to often forget what I wanted to do. Jasper responded to my confusion by making the choice for me, leaving his activity to lead me to where he imagined I wanted to go.

It was a bittersweet time for me, because although I was serene and happy with my new home, I felt anxious to do and see as much as I could. A growing uneasiness was unsettling my meditations, even waking me up from peaceful and nostalgic dreams. My masters noted this and became troubled and perplexed. They took me to the vet, who told them the same thing we'd heard in White Rock. And they prayed.

The days were like late fall days in the west. This was the warm southeast, but the locals told us that this winter was unusually cold. The temperature dropped at night, but we were cozy in our lovely home and we all snuggled together.

Quite unexpectedly one evening, I came to the decision that I should not despair. I had received more

happiness and love than I had ever imagined possible. My life was rich and filled with warm remembrances. I had cared for the Mistress for many years, and I knew that Mr. Mike would never allow anything to happen to her. Jasper stood loyally beside me during my affliction, and would accompany my loved ones in my stead. My faith in the masters and my conviction of their love and abilities embraced my soul. A shiver of peace warmed my heart as I cherished the thought that they were loved and led by their Lord. Tonight I would sleep like a contented kitten at peace in her new home.

The Rainbow Bridge
by
The Mistress

Kiska went downhill very quickly. One day she stopped eating solid food. The next day she had difficulty jumping off the bed to the floor. As her thirst for water increased, her times of rest decreased. Her back legs began to wobble as she made the long walk from the family room to the laundry room for her water. We moved it next to the sofa where she slept, but she wandered about on her spindly legs anyway, disoriented and restless. She seemed to be on a mission, and it was up to me to understand what that was.

Because I was not working, I was home with Kiska and could watch her closely. She wanted to go out-doors more than ever before, even in the rain. Kiska had always avoided the rain, so this was another dis-turbing sign. One afternoon as my husband and I were putting things away in the garage, Kiska asked to join us. We let her out and watched her wander to the large side yard, where she sat down to rest. Not even three minutes later, she was out of sight! We both rushed down to the lake's edge near the place she had been sitting, and found her balanced on a narrow tree branch which jetted out from the shore. She cried for help when she saw us, and we gently raised her off the branch. She was too weak to crawl up the embank-ment and settled in my arms to be carried home.

As I watched Kiska standing over her water dish, unsteady on her feet and looking confused, I realized that she was losing her dignity. Kiska had always been proud and alert and now she seemed to be look-ing to me for an explanation of her situation. I talked to her and told her how much I loved her. I asked her to let me know when it was time to help her leave us. I quietly asked her to prepare me for her journey and show me how to be brave.

Jasper kept a close watch over Kiska as well. He

curled up around her fragile body to keep her warm. He groomed her constantly, cleaning out her ears and other places she was having trouble reaching. As she lost more weight, her little face was beginning to look unkempt. She acquired a wide-eyed vacant look, and finally we smelled a faint musty odor about her. Jasper escorted her and protected her most of the day. But once again she slipped through our guard and disappeared. I knew immediately to look on that tree branch in the water. When I got to her she was trying to turn around on it, and was slipping into the shallow water at the lake's edge. Her feet were soaked and she was crying a sad, plaintive protest. I scooped her into my arms and sobbed.

For several days after she stopped eating solid food she would accept tuna fish, clam juice and a bite of wet cat food. Then she totally stopped eating, drinking only water. Her strength visibly ebbed, but she still insisted on wobbling around the house and outdoors. All of her bones were showing yet she seemed to grasp energy from determination. I drew her into my arms and asked her again if she wanted me to help her find peace and rest. This time, she gave me a long, loving, very lucid look, closed her eyes, and began to purr. To my great sorrow, I had my answer.

The next morning I spent every moment with Kiska, allowing her to come and go as much as she wanted. We walked the entire area of our new home and property. She rested often and I sat with her. She wanted to go back down to the same tree branch projecting from the lake's edge, and I helped her off once more. Her steps were slow and labored, but she wanted to see everything one more time. She seemed calm and I tried valiantly to mirror her peace for her sake. Even on that day she noticed my tears and curled up on my lap to comfort me.

I carried her in her favorite blanket to the car and we drove the few miles to the vet. This was the first time in her nineteen years that Kiska did not object to riding in the car. For some reason, that gave me some peace. When we arrived, one of the veterinarian's cats meandered over to meet Kiska. He licked her face, and she licked him back. Dr. Lisa and I discussed the alternatives and watched Kiska walk slowly around the room. Then she left me alone to make my final decision. I knew what I had to do, and so did my beloved cat. As bravely as I could, I embraced her and told her how much she meant to me, how I loved her and how she had enriched our lives. I spoke to her of Heaven, of seeing Canica again, and of a new world to explore.

Dr. Lisa returned and we laid Kiska in her blanket on the table. She didn't protest; she was ready. Both of us spoke soothingly to her as the needle went into her back leg. Brave little Kiska did not even flinch. I held her tiny head in my right hand, and with tears streaming down my cheeks invited her to enjoy a deep sleep, with very happy dreams. Dr. Lisa spoke to her of peace and rest and happiness. It was a liberating yet heart-wrenching time as Kiska quietly and peacefully left her earthly body. I felt the exact moment that her heart stopped beating, and for a brief moment, I met her soul.

The Rainbow Bridge Story

Author Unknown

Just this side of Heaven is a place called Rainbow Bridge. When an animal dies that has been especially close to someone here, that pet goes to Rainbow Bridge. There are meadows and hills for all of our special friends so they can run and play together. There is plenty of food, water and sunshine, and our friends are warm and comfortable. All the animals who had been ill and old are restored to health and vigor; those who were hurt or maimed are made whole and strong again, just as we remember them in our dreams of days and times gone by.

The animals are happy and content, except for one small thing: they each miss someone very special to them, someone who had to be left behind.

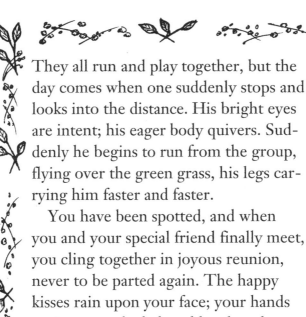

They all run and play together, but the day comes when one suddenly stops and looks into the distance. His bright eyes are intent; his eager body quivers. Suddenly he begins to run from the group, flying over the green grass, his legs carrying him faster and faster.

You have been spotted, and when you and your special friend finally meet, you cling together in joyous reunion, never to be parted again. The happy kisses rain upon your face; your hands again caress the beloved head, and you look once more into the trusting eyes of your pet, so long gone from your life but never absent from your heart.

Then you cross Rainbow Bridge together . . .

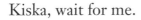

Kiska, wait for me.

Until that day,
The Mistress

Burial

We buried Kiska in our back yard by the light of the first star. Mike dug her grave under an old oak tree right next to the lake. Jasper hovered closely, but I sensed it was too sorrowful and upsetting to let him near the box where she lay. After we put her in the ground, Mike and I prayed for her soul to be lifted up. Jasper watched us from a distance. We covered her grave with Spanish moss and mournfully returned to our house.

The next morning we noticed that the first camellia of the year had blossomed on a backyard bush, as if in tribute to Kiska. In a craft store in the Village, we discovered a beautifully carved wooden angel holding a basket, meant to be a birdfeeder. I filled the basket with water, picked the graceful white camellia and set it in the angel's basket.

We positioned the angel at the head of Kiska's grave to watch over her body. Her soul, we knew, had left the box and was enjoying eternal freedom. Then we left Jasper alone with Kiska's spirit.

19

Kiska's Crossing
by
Mr. Mike

As I went to sleep, I began to dream. In my dream I left the table and jumped back into the kitty carrier. The Mistress was crying, but was comforted by the people she was with as I fell asleep. She left the building with the kitty carrier and a box and placed both in the car. I thought it strange that she did not notice I was there.

Upon arrival at the house, the Mistress took a shovel from the garage and began to dig a hole under the large oak tree in the back yard. After a time, Mr. Mike arrived to complete the hole. Jasper, sitting on his back haunches in his prairie dog pose, watched the whole scene. I trotted over to him. He quivered and his eyes opened wide. I told him that I was going to a new home, and as we had discussed, he would now be the cat in charge of the Mistress and Mr. Mike. Jasper then went to the other side of the yard and rested on all fours with his back rounded as he contemplated these responsibilities.

The Mistress and Mr. Mike placed the box in the hole and covered the box with dirt, under the first star of the night, illuminated by the light of the full Georgian moon.

Before I fell asleep, I heard the friendly stranger tell the Mistress not to be surprised if they heard my meows or my footsteps. I knew the Mistress would remember me forever and would not need to hear me. I was not so sure about Mr. Mike as he did not always give me the total adoration I deserved. So I walked by an open doorway and Mr. Mike, being a sensitive human, looked over his shoulder like he heard my footsteps. Later, while Mr. Mike was working in the garage I let out a meow. Mr. Mike looked up in total surprise and with a sad half smile said, "Yes Kiska, I know you're here." I knew he would also remember me forever.

Finally I meandered through the house one more

time. I found the Mistress and smiled at her with my eyes. At that point a light appeared and I heard my name being called in cat language by what sounded like Canica's voice. The voice was telling me to come to my new home!

Epilogue

I stepped through the light into my new home. I was met at a gate by Canica, Mother and a man in a white robe. Canica said, "Mother and I are here to welcome you to your new home. You've done well with Miss Cassandra, Miss Ticiana and the Mistress, and in time you will get to snuggle with them again. Here we get to watch over them and help their guardian angels. In the meantime, this is our new Master, whom we call the Shepherd. But right now, your brothers and sisters are waiting for you to join us in a race and some boxing and . . ."

Homage to Kiska

*Those we hold most dear never truly leave
us . . . they live on in the kindness they
showed, the comfort they shared, and the
love they brought into our hearts."*
　　　　　　　　　—Author Unknown

After her passing, we received an outpouring of condolences and tributes to Kiska, both written and spo-
ken. In heartfelt appreciation to all of you, and in
honor of her, we are including many of them in the
last chapter of Kiska's final book. If your e-mail or
letter has not been included, please know that we are
grateful and very thankful for your loving thought-
fulness. Unfortunately, in the interest of space and
diversification, we found it essential to edit. Thank
you to everyone who helped us through our sorrow.

Dear Kiska,

You will always have a special place in my heart, as you were my first-born kitty cat. No cat will ever take your place, especially cuddling under the covers with me at night. Every cat I've had since you pales in comparison and none will let me keep them under the covers for more than three seconds. Your purr, your beautiful eyes, and your tiny size: I will cherish all those memories of my very special kitty.

I've told Marlena that you are in Kitty Heaven and that it's a good place because it's close to where Jesus lives. It seems to satisfy her knowing that you are in some comfort and peace even if she cannot hold you anymore. You made many a child happy by letting them all share a little part of you. But don't forget all the adults whose lives you touched even more.

We will miss you very much but we know that you are looking down from Kitty Heaven with a special smile and a strong, comforting purr that you have never had before.

Much love,
Miss Cassandra—your first
mama
St. Paul, Minnesota

Mom and Mike,

I am so sorry for what has happened! I simply couldn't hold back my tears today when I heard the news. Kiska is a huge part of our lives and I know this is very hard for you. I'm glad you have Jasper (and he has you). Hang in there.

Love you very much!
>
> Miss Ticiana
> Portland, Oregon

I send my condolences to you both. Kiska was much loved and she lived a full life. I think that the next book we do should be in her memory.
>
> Naomi Marie Weiler
> Victoria, B.C., Canada

We just want to let you know that we have been thinking of you and Jasper since we heard of Kiska's passing. You will miss the physical presence of the exceptional kitty that she was, but she will be in your hearts forever. We know this because of our experience with Oscar. He is still here with us.
>
> Love you,
> Wendy and Don Bauer
> San Francisco, California

I knew that Kiska was sick, because Mom had told me. I am so sorry about her death. She was a cat for all seasons and all places! I can picture her in Mexico with the girls being little and your life being very Mexican. Then I remember her in San Diego, when I brought baby Marshall and he tried to touch her and she hid! Then when I was down there once she slept in the waterbed with me and did "happy feet" before she settled down. I think I was pregnant then, and the waterbed felt so good on my big belly! I think Kiska liked being near me and the baby inside. Then of course we had our various visits to White Rock when we totally freaked her out with all of our noise and young children! But she was a trooper, and certainly lived an incredibly long time. We are all sad for you. Thank goodness for Jasper. Plant some colorful flowers around her grave, such as pansies or primroses.

Much love to you both,
Rebecca Bauer
Portland, Oregon

I'm here on quiet, rainy Friday and wept when reading your e-mail. It sounded so much like Bebe who also had kidney failure—although I do not know where she chose to rest—her spirit lives on as does the infamous Kiska—she ended her life on earth fresh from a journey—adding depth to the last chapter. Animals are so good at seeping into the deepest parts of who we are and she has certainly shared the highs and lows with you—but take comfort that she had a good life and was totally loved. I know you miss her terribly but know that a new cat will enter your life at the appropriate time.

Love,
Barbie Stinchfield
Santa Monica, California

I was so sorry to hear of your tremendous loss. Kiska's memories will always be immortalized in your heartfelt words that others will share. I know that Kiska and Zombie are enjoying their new friendship as they spend their time together . . . and wait . . . at Rainbow Bridge.

Wynne Toba
Bellingham, Washington

I'm so sorry about Kiska. I'm writing with tears in my eyes. You have so many good memories of your little girl and thanks to Pam's hard work, she'll forever be alive in her books. Kiska could not have gotten a better home and fellow furry friend than what you two gave her. Theo and I send our love and deepest sympathy.

> Joy Lang
> Vancouver, B.C., Canada

Kiska's legend will live long in the hearts of all who knew her and all who read about her wonderful journey through life. The tribute you have given her will bring peace and joy to many children and adults alike everywhere.

> Love,
> June Barens
> White Rock, B.C., Canada

I was sad to hear about Kiska. It's hard to lose a dear little pet and I feel for you both. I remembered that she was beyond ancient, and think it's amazing that she made the trip across country in decent shape, especially considering the diagnosis she received before you left. She was truly the International Cat. Nice though that she lived long enough to be buried in your new spot—a considerate cat, too.

> Love,
> Janet Gouin
> Port Angeles, Washington

I want to say how sad and sorry I felt that dear Kiska has moved on. You will miss her so much but more than you, Jasper will grieve. It's been awhile now so maybe he's over it. Animals have a way of dealing with death as matter of fact and after a short grieving period, they seem to go on. When we lost our baby donkey, Gary and I grieved for about six months. I though how silly, why do I keep crying whenever I think of Moonbeam. Gradually, in time, I came to realize what a wonderful gift we had received to have that kind of relationship with another of God's creatures. I felt blessed because I knew what we had shared was special—a gift from above.

Your love for Kiska was very special and it was that love that you gave her that made her into such a unique kitty. I do believe that the lucky animals that receive the kind of love that you and we give them make them become the best of what they can be. They possess unique qualities because of their close relationship to their masters and also because they feel loved and have that confident air about them.

The difference is with the loss of Kiska, you are not alone in your grieving. Everyone who read your books will feel a loss because we felt like we knew her. Thank you, Pam, for allowing us a glimpse of Kiska's wonderful personality. We all feel the loss but especially you and the girls because you went through so much together. You must have received many condolences from her many fans. I feel privileged to have met her— for a little kitty, she touched so many lives.

Eleanor and Gary Livingstone
Surrey, B.C., Canada

Losing such a special friend after such a long time is always difficult. I like to think that Kiska and TJ are playing in Kitty Heaven as I type this letter. Isn't it weird how they let you know they are going to die and they're okay with it? Cats are the best ever, aren't they?

Love,
Shannon Stewart
Ottawa, Ontario, Canada

So very sorry and what a beautiful eulogy!

> Love,
> Terry Patterson
> Lauderdale by the Sea, Florida

I was very sorry to hear about Kiska. I pray that the Lord will comfort you during this difficult time. Mona and I want to express our condolences. Though we never met her in person, it seems like we knew her through her books. In time, may the Lord bring a new kitty into your lives that will be a spiritual offspring of your dear and beloved Kiska. I know that she was unique and that she will never be replaced. May the big oak be a reminder of her permanence in your hearts.

> In His love,
> Herb and Mona Porter
> Bellingham, Washington

We know how much joy Kiska has brought to you and your family and her many fans. Isn't it truly wonderful how much we are able to love our animals and how they really do become part of our family? I'm so glad that she made it to your new home and that she did not suffer. Thanks for sharing such a difficult and special time with us.

> Sonny and Debbie Hryniuk
> White Rock, B.C., Canada

I'm so sorry for your great loss. Mary and I will remember Kiska and both of you in our prayers. Her memories will live on with the books.

> Louie and Mary Semon
> San Diego, California

My heart goes out to you over the loss of your beloved Kiska. She will live, not only in your hearts forever, but also in the hearts of all the people whose lives she's touched with her books. Her spirit will always be with you. My dear Mikey King of Dogs is always with me and sometimes even gives me signs that he's present. It's really quite amazing.

Kiska most certainly was loved and had a very special life, but undoubtedly you will miss her tremendously. Please take care and know that I'm thinking of you.

> Georgeanne Irvine
> San Diego, California

What a touching tribute to a precious being in our respective lives. Those of us who have animal children understand the pleasures and good feelings they bring out in humans and the often-used term "unconditional love" they show us over and over again! We understand fully and share your sorrow at this time!

Wayne and Lori Chmilar
White Rock, B.C., Canada

You have my deepest sympathy for Kiska's death. I remember how much you loved her, and now you have immortalized her in your lovely books. I trust and I hope—that your beautiful eulogy will be part of your last book about her. I never met her, but she was still very real to me.

Bobbie Cassidy
San Diego, California

I am so sorry to hear about Kiska's passing. What a beautiful memorial you wrote for her! I was both saddened and uplifted by your loving words. I hope these days find you filled with happier thoughts and memories. Some people never understand or get to experience how much joy and love a pet can bring to a family. We are the lucky ones who have those memories and are bettered by them.

Kerri and Jim Janoewicz
Hamburg, New York

So sorry to hear about Kiska. Having had several kitties of my own, I know how attached one becomes to them. They are each individuals with loving spirits of their own. Kiska had a good life with you all and is now resting peacefully in your new home. She'll guard your backyard. We'll miss hearing about the adventures of Kiska. Now Jasper will have to take over. Of course, Kiska can communicate with Jasper from Kitty Heaven. I firmly believe that spirits live on.

Joy Anstey
Vancouver, B.C., Canada

Sorry to hear about Kiska but her legend will live on thanks to the books and website.

Dale Liikala

Crane Lake, Minnesota

Kiska's most enthusiastic fans, the school children, did not know about her demise at the time of this printing. We chose not to post it on her website, allowing the children to discover her passing through her words in her final book. Miss Ticiana and I did a presentation to one elementary school here in St. Simons Island in March 2001, where we imparted the sad news. This note of appreciation illustrates what we feel is the heartfelt reaction of children everywhere.

Dear Mrs. Ticiana and Mrs. Mueller,

I'm sorry that Kiska died, but she is in a safe place.

Sincerely,
Sharkira Gammage
St. Simons Elementary School
St. Simons, Georgia

Afterword

Hello. My name is Emmeline Valentina and I'm a kitten. The Mistress told me I was born on Valentine Day, so now I'm three months old. Jasper says I am old enough to write.

I live in a large house with many trees around it. The masters let me go outside for awhile each afternoon, and Jasper watches over me. Sometimes I miss my mother and my brothers and sisters. Jasper explained to me that lucky kittens find homes with humans when the time is right. I was really lucky because there was already a big cat waiting for me in this new home.

There are two kind humans who live in this house and love me. The Mistress stays home a lot and swings with me in the back yard. Mr. Mike goes to work, but when he comes home he plays ball and string games with me. Mostly, I play with Jasper. I like to box him or attack him from behind when he's sleeping. He is big, but he would never hurt me. Usually he lets me win.

One day I will be able to explore the whole back yard and go down to the lake behind the house. Maybe I can even go up the street with Jasper when he patrols the neighborhood. He is teaching me how to be safe. Yesterday I ran up a tree and then forgot how to come down. Jasper helped me so now I will remember. The noise of the garage door frightens me and I stay far away from it. Another danger could be the big white dog who barks at us from next door. One time she even chased Jasper up a tree!

They have told me that another cat lived with them for many years. Her name was Kiska, and they love her very much. She was really old when she left them for Kitty Heaven. Sometimes they forget and call me Kiska. I don't mind.

One day Jasper took me to the back yard and showed me Kiska's gravesite. At first we felt very sad out there, but then Jasper told me about the naughty and funny things they did, and we felt happy. The Mistress told me that Kiska talked to her and together they wrote their stories into books. Mr. Mike showed me the books with pictures of Kiska and Jasper on the back. Last night the Mistress said that she and Mr. Mike would read me the books. I am looking forward to that.

Hmm, do you suppose I could be clever enough to write a book?

About the Author

Pamela Bauer Mueller was raised in Oregon and graduated from Lewis and Clark College in Portland, Oregon. She worked as a flight attendant for Pan American Airlines before moving to Mexico City, where she lived for eighteen years. Pamela is bicultural as well as bilingual. She has worked as a commercial model, actress, and an English and Spanish language instructor during her years in Mexico. After returning to the United States, Pamela worked for twelve years as a U.S. Customs inspector. After serving six years in San Diego, California, she was selected to work a foreign assignment in Vancouver, British Columbia, Canada. Pamela took an early retirement from U.S. Customs to follow her husband, Michael, who received an instructor position at the Federal Law Enforcement Training Center in Brunswick, Georgia. They reside on St. Simons Island, Georgia with their cats, Jasper and Emmeline. Pamela completed the Kiska Trilogy in Georgia, and now looks forward to writing historical novels in her new southern home.

About the Illustrator

Naomi Marie Weiler was born and raised in the city of Victoria, British Columbia, Canada. This is her third collaboration with Pam and Kiska about the adventures of Kiska, Jasper, Canica and the whole family. She is presently studying theatre set and costume design at the University of Victoria. She plans to continue her studies in Montreal, Quebec, Canada in the near future. She would like to dedicate this book to Bobby the Bunny, Bandit the "Terror," Richard the Clumsy King and every other animal with whom we share this precious planet.